Sister Magic

Mabel on the Move

We think you will also enjoy these books
by Anne Mazer

Sister Magic

Sister Magic

Mabel on the Move

BY ANNE MAZER

ILLUSTRATED BY BILL BROWN

SCHOLASTIC INC.

New York Toronto London Auckland Sydney
Mexico City New Delhi Hong Kong Buenos Aires

To my friend Mary

ISBN-13: 978-0-439-87251-5
ISBN-10: 0-439-87251-0

12 11 10 9 8 7 6 5 4 3 2 1   9 10 11 12 13/0
                                                    40

Printed in the U.S.A.
First printing, March 2009

Chapter One

Mabel carried piles of neatly folded clothes to the bed where an empty suitcase lay open.

Then she consulted her list.

1. *Pack suitcase. Use special packing bags.*

She took a plastic bag and carefully placed a pile of folded shorts inside.

She pressed out all the air from the bag and zipped it tightly.

Now her shorts wouldn't wrinkle. And neither would any of her other clothes. Mabel hated crumpled clothes.

Mabel put her T-shirts, underwear, and bathing suits into the packing bags.

She slipped her sandals and water shoes into drawstring pouches.

Then she tightened all the caps on her shampoo and lotion.

She put her toothbrush in a special travel case.

Everything was organized. It made Mabel feel calm and in charge.

She looked at her list again.

2. *Bring addressed, stamped postcards to send to friends while on vacation.*

Yes, Mabel had already bought postcards to send to her friends. They had pictures of fruit, baby animals, and goofy people on them. They didn't have pictures of their destination. But did that really matter, anyway?

Her mother thought that was crazy.

"Why don't you wait until we get there?" she asked.

"But what if there aren't any postcards?" Mabel asked.

"There are always postcards," her mother assured her.

"Always?" Mabel repeated. "What if we get stranded on a desert island? Or get caught in a tropical storm?"

Her mother laughed. "We're visiting your cousins. They live in the country, sure, but it's only three miles to town."

But Mabel believed in being prepared.

If she really thought ahead, she'd write the postcards *now*. Then all she'd have to do would be to post them in a mailbox.

Having fun. Wish you were here. Violet is a pest. Love, Mabel

No matter where they were, and what they were doing, those words would always be true.

Mabel let out a sigh. She couldn't wait to be on vacation. She couldn't wait to see her cousins.

But she wished she didn't have to be stuck in the backseat for two days with her annoying little sister.

Thinking of Violet brought her to the next item on her list:

3. Pack a bag of games, books, music, and other stuff for car. Be sure to take extra things for Violet.

Violet would have her own bag, of course. But it was smart to have a few things to share with her.

She always wanted whatever Mabel had.

Mabel took out a backpack.

She packed it with paperback books, games, brainteasers, puzzles, her portable music player, snack bars, and stuffed toys.

Then she added stickers, coloring books,

markers, and a few of her old toys for Violet.

Mabel zipped up the backpack and put it next to the suitcase on the bed. She was almost ready to leave.

She felt a shiver of excitement.

It was a long trip, but they were breaking it up. Tonight they were staying in a hotel.

By tomorrow evening, they'd be at their cousins' house.

There were two girls, Zoe and Mya, who were exactly the same ages as Mabel and Violet.

Mabel didn't know them very well. She hadn't seen them in three years. They were her father's relatives.

Mabel glanced at her list. There was only one item left.

4. Give Violet the Talk.

Mabel sighed deeply.

It didn't matter how many times Mabel

gave Violet "the Talk." In the end, Violet did what she wanted.

But Mabel had to go through with it. There was no one else to warn, caution, and protect Violet.

Mabel was the only one in the family who knew about her little sister's magic.

Chapter Two

"You mustn't use your magic this week," Mabel warned her little sister.

"Why not?" Violet demanded. She was still in pajamas. She hadn't even gotten out of bed.

Mabel sighed. She had been awake for hours. But it was never the right time to argue with Violet. "You know why not."

They were leaving in an hour. This was Mabel's last chance to prepare her little sister for their trip.

"Magic is fun," Violet persisted. "Why can't I use it?"

"Magic is dangerous," Mabel said.

"There are going to be too many people around. Our cousins, for a start."

"I'll be careful," Violet promised.

"No," Mabel said.

"Very, *very* careful," Violet said.

"It's way too risky," Mabel said. "What if Mom finds out?"

Their mother had grown up with magic. Uncle Vartan, their mother's little brother, had magic, too. That should have made things easier for Violet and Mabel.

Instead, it made them worse.

It had ruined their mother's childhood. Now she didn't want to talk, think, or hear about magic. Ever.

She would be horribly upset if she knew that Violet had magic. It might ruin her life forever.

"You can't wreck Mom and Dad's vacation," Mabel said. "Or mine. Or yours."

Violet crossed her eyes.

"Listen to me," Mabel pleaded. "This is important."

"That's what you always say," Violet said. She jumped out of bed and began to turn cartwheels on her bedroom floor.

Why did she *get the magic?* Mabel thought for the millionth time. It was *so* unfair.

Mabel was the careful sister. The responsible one.

Violet, on the other hand, was wild, messy, and careless.

"I want to have a fun vacation, Violet," Mabel said. "I want a magic vacation, too."

"You mean lots of magic?" Violet said, tumbling over the carpet.

"No! I mean a vacation *from* magic." Mabel took a deep breath. "Do you understand?"

"Yup," Violet said, standing on her hands.

Mabel hoped it was true. But she couldn't exactly trust Violet.

"Time to get dressed," Mabel said. "We're leaving soon."

Mabel · went back to her room. She brought her suitcase and backpack downstairs.

Her father was loading up the car.

He packed suitcases, inflatable rafts, life jackets, bicycles, folding chairs, tents, toys, coolers, and snorkeling gear into the trunk.

"We could survive a couple of months in

the wilderness with all this stuff," he grumbled.

Mabel tried to look sympathetic. But she was glad that her family was so well prepared.

"Do you think we forgot anything?" her father asked. "Like a lawn tractor or the bedroom furniture?"

Mabel shook her head.

"Thank goodness," he said.

"Is it almost time to leave?" Mabel couldn't wait to be on the road.

Her father checked the time. "Your mother was supposed to be ready ten minutes ago," he said. "Sandra?"

"We're coming!" his wife called.

Mabel's father slammed the trunk shut. Then he got into the front seat and put his key in the ignition.

Mabel got into the seat behind her father. She buckled up her seat belt. She checked her reflection in a mirror.

Her hair was neat and combed. Her face was clean and shiny. Her clothes matched and her shoelaces were tied in double knots.

She was ready.

Violet and her mother hurried out of the house. Her mother took the passenger seat next to her husband.

Mabel winced as Violet got into the backseat next to her. It hurt to even look at her little sister.

Violet wore green plaid shorts, a tangerine polka-dot T-shirt, and purple rubber boots.

"Curls," Violet said mysteriously.

"What?" Mabel said.

In answer, Violet threw her open tote bag onto the seat. Dolls, books, and games tumbled onto the floor.

Mabel sighed. It was going to be a long trip.

Violet sat down and buckled her seat belt. Then she turned and grinned at Mabel.

Mabel began to smile, too. But then she froze.

Violet's hair was slowly turning color.

First it was curly and light brown. Then it was a pale, glowing pink. The pink turned to purple, and then to a brilliant orange.

Crazy, colorful curls sprang out from Violet's head.

Mabel made frantic motions for Violet to stop.

Violet only smiled. Her orange curls began to cascade down her shoulders like a cape.

In the front seat, their parents were consulting a map.

What would they say if they saw Violet's orange hair? What would they say if they saw it growing so fast?

What if Violet decided to turn *Mabel's* hair green or gold or magenta?

Mabel kicked Violet in the shin.

"Mom!!!" Violet screeched. "Mabel kicked me!"

"You know why," Mabel said under her breath. She was relieved to see that Violet's hair had miraculously gone back to normal.

"We haven't even left the driveway and already you two are fighting," their mother scolded.

Mabel hung her head — even though it was really Violet's fault.

"I want peace and quiet," their mother said. She folded the map and put it in the glove compartment.

Their father removed the key from the ignition. "We can't leave until you both promise that you'll try to get along on this trip."

"Girls?" their mother said.

"I'll try," Mabel said.

"Oh, all right," Violet said.

It was sort of a "yes." It would have to do.

Their father started the car and began to back slowly out of the driveway.

Chapter Three

"I have to go to the bathroom," Violet announced.

"Again?" her mother said. "You just went."

Mabel glanced at the juice boxes littering the floor of the backseat. She had warned her little sister not to drink so much, but did Violet listen to her?

She had also warned her about not using her magic. And look what she had done to her hair.

Happily, that was all over now. Mabel hoped that Violet was done with magic for a while.

"We won't be able to stop right away," their father said.

Violet bit her lip. "I really, really, *really* have to go."

Her mother looked anxious. "We'll pull off at the next exit," she said. "Hold on, Violet."

"Can I go at the side of the road?" Violet asked.

"Violet!" Mabel said.

Their father glanced at the many lanes of speeding traffic. "It's way too dangerous," he said. "You'll have to wait, Violet."

Violet squirmed in her seat.

"Mabel, can you help?" her mother begged. "Do something to distract her."

Mabel sat up straighter. She loved to help. She pulled out a deck of cards. "Do you want to play Go Fish, Violet?"

"That's a dumb game." Violet grabbed the cards and began to shuffle. Then she let go of them. They fluttered into the air like birds.

Violet laughed in delight.

Mabel glanced at her parents. Her mother was fiddling with the radio. Her father was focused on the road.

She nudged Violet with her elbow. "Cut it out!" she hissed.

The cards came tumbling down.

Mabel picked them up. She zipped the cards into her backpack.

"How about if I read you a story?" Mabel said. "I brought lots of good books."

"No story." Violet folded her arms across her chest and crossed her legs. She looked like a bright, colorful, stubborn pretzel.

"All right. What about Alphabet?"

It was a car game their father had taught them. They each watched signs and billboards for words that began with the letters of the alphabet.

Violet didn't answer.

"You *do* know your alphabet, don't you?" Mabel challenged.

"Of course I do!"

Violet leaned toward the window and began to scan the signs. "I see an *A*!"

"*A* for area," Mabel read, as the highway sign flashed past. "Rest area thirty-seven miles away."

"*B! C! D! E!*" Violet called.

"'Carrie's Best Diner'," Mabel read to her. "'Exit 21.'"

"*F!*" Violet cried. "Five. Just like me!"

"You're reading,'" Mabel complimented her.

"*G! H!*" Violet was bouncing with excitement. "Gas. Hotel!"

Their mother turned around. "Great, honey. I didn't know you knew so many words."

Maybe Mabel could teach Violet some new ones. Her parents would be so proud of her.

"Where are the *I*'s?" Violet asked.

"Nothing yet," Mabel said.

"I don't want to wait," Violet said. "Can't we just skip the *I*?"

"That would be cheating," Mabel said.

"So?" Violet said.

Mabel shook her head. "You know better than that, Violet."

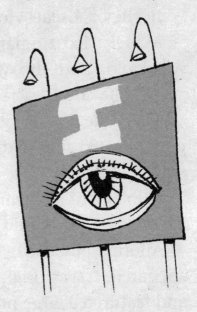

A billboard with a huge staring eye appeared on the side of the road. It was accompanied by the single letter *I*.

"*I!*" Violet yelled triumphantly.

"That's a strange kind of billboard," their father said.

Mabel looked hard at her little sister.

"Maybe it's a new kind of advertisement," their mother suggested. "Or one of those personal statements."

"You can't get more personal than a giant eye," their father said.

In the backseat, Violet smirked.

Mabel tried to glare at her. But Violet was looking out the window.

"J!" she cried.

This time it was a green polka-dotted sign with a single white letter.

"Violet," Mabel warned in a low voice. "Don't do this."

Another billboard appeared. It was bright pink and featured a large purple cake with an orange letter *K*.

"K!" Violet said.

"Cake begins with *C*, not *K*," Mabel told her.

"So?" Violet said. "It has the letter *K* right on top!"

There was nothing Mabel could say to that. But the sign was *so* Violet. How could her parents not see the connection?

"Wow, that's a colorful one," their father said.

"Do you think it's an alphabet festival?" their mother asked.

"L!" Violet cried as another crazy bill-board flashed by.

She pointed to a large elephant holding the letter *L* in his trunk.

As the family watched, the elephant trumpeted loudly. The letter *L* clattered to the ground.

Mabel buried her face in her hands.

"Great special effects!" their father cried.

"Or maybe it's a creativity contest," their mother said. "But why don't they use a llama or a lion?"

"I like elephants," Violet said.

"Are we almost there?" Mabel asked desperately.

"What do you think they'll have for the letter *M*?" her father said. "A billboard with Mabel's face?"

Violet's eyes lit up.

"*M!*" Mabel yelled loudly. " 'Exit one-half *m*ile.' We're almost at the stop."

"Good eye, Mabel," her father said. "I might have missed that. Do you still need a rest stop, Violet?"

"*N* is for no," Violet began. "*O* is for . . ."

"Okay!" Mabel interrupted. "Of course we need a rest stop."

Mabel led Violet into the ladies' room. "No floating over the toilet seat," she hissed.

A woman in a pink polka-dot shirt gave them a strange look.

Violet began to sing the letters of the alphabet. "A, B, C, D, E, F, G . . ." she sang in a high voice.

Mabel banged on the door of the stall. "Cut it out, Violet," she said.

"Don't you like my singing?" Violet said.

Letters floated up in the air from above Violet's stall.

"Violet," Mabel warned.

The letters disappeared. Violet emerged, looking smug.

As she washed and dried her hands, Mabel stared at her reflection in the mirror.

I'm going to have to watch Violet every single minute of this vacation, she said to herself. *I can't let her out of my sight.*

It wasn't going to be easy, relaxing, or fun.

But Mabel was the only one who could do it.

Chapter Four

Mabel's mother shook her shoulder.

"What?" Mabel said.

"Time to get up. We're at the hotel."

She opened her eyes. It was dark. Her head was resting at an odd angle. Her arms and legs felt cramped.

"I can't wake Violet up," her mother whispered.

"Do you want me to try?" Mabel offered.

Her mother shook her head. "Your father will carry her inside. As soon as he gets back."

"Where is he?" Mabel asked.

"Checking in. Do you have your

toothbrush and a clean change of clothes?" her mother asked.

"I have everything," Mabel said. She rubbed her eyes and yawned.

Her mother patted her arm. "Of course you do."

A few minutes later, the whole family was stumbling sleepily up the stairs.

Mabel's mother put the card key into the lock. It flashed green. She pushed down on the handle and opened the door.

"Room sweet room," their father said.

"Room *suite* room," their mother repeated.

"Why are you repeating what Dad said?" Mabel asked.

Her parents laughed.

Mabel frowned. She didn't understand why that was funny.

"'Suite' is pronounced the same as 'sweet,'" her father explained.

"We took a suite of two rooms," her mother said. "There's a bedroom for your father and me. And a living room with a pullout couch for you and Violet."

Mabel stared at her in dismay. This suite wasn't sweet for *her*.

"You didn't tell me I had to sleep in a bed with Violet," she said.

"It's queen-size," her mother said, as if that made it better.

"Violet kicks and talks in her sleep," Mabel said. "I want my own bed."

Her father sighed. "I'm sorry, pumpkin. The front desk messed up. You were supposed to get a cot. But there's no one to make it right this late."

"You have a television." Her mother tried to soothe her. "You and Violet can watch cartoons early tomorrow morning before we leave."

"I hate television." Mabel was getting crankier by the minute.

Anyone would be in a bad mood if they were faced with sharing a mattress with Violet.

"It's late, we've had a long trip, and we're tired," her mother said. "You can share for just one night."

"No, I can't," Mabel said.

Her mother sighed. Then she slipped off Violet's purple boots and socks.

She eased a nightgown over Violet's head and lifted her into bed.

Violet rolled into the middle. She yanked the blankets into a knot. A small snore came out of her mouth.

"See?" Mabel cried. "She always takes up all the space."

She stomped into the bathroom to brush her teeth.

When she came out again, her parents had gone into their bedroom.

Violet was still in the middle.

"They don't care," Mabel said to herself. She climbed into bed and lay on the edge.

She knew it was late and everyone was tired. But that didn't help any. Mabel fumed until she fell asleep.

In the middle of the night, Mabel woke up.

A strange purple light filled the room. It was accompanied by a low humming noise.

No one was next to her in the bed.

"Violet?" Mabel whispered. She climbed out of bed to see if her sister was in the bathroom.

She wasn't.

Mabel looked up, half expecting to see Violet flying through the hotel room in her nightgown.

She wasn't.

She peeked into the closet, hoping that Violet wasn't changing bathing suits into suits of armor.

She wasn't.

There was a noise from the corner.

Mabel looked down. Violet was curled up in a blanket on the floor.

"There you are!" Mabel cried. "What are you doing? Why aren't you in bed?"

"I'm scared," Violet said in a small voice. "My bear isn't here."

Mabel crouched next to her sister. "Don't worry," she said. "We probably left him in the car. He'll be okay. And I'm here, too."

"You were sleeping."

"Not anymore." Mabel held out her hand. "Come back to bed."

Violet glanced fearfully around the hotel room. "When did we get here?" she asked. "Where are Mom and Dad?"

"They're right here, behind that door," Mabel reassured her. "And if you make the purple light go away, I'll tell you a story."

Sometimes her little sister was a magician. And sometimes she was just a little girl.

Chapter Five

As the car turned onto their cousins' road, Mabel began to get nervous.

They had lots of exciting things planned for their vacation.

They were going to a lake. They were going to a botanical garden. They were going to sleep in a tent.

But Mabel hadn't seen her cousins for years.

She knew that Zoe liked sports and reading. She played soccer, baseball, lacrosse, and tennis.

But what was she like? Was she organized like Mabel? Or messy like Violet?

Was she friendly or stuck-up? Was she energetic or lazy? Shy or social?

What if she and Mabel couldn't stand each other? What if they didn't like doing the same things?

They'd be stuck together for a week. They'd have to make the best of it.

And then there were Mya and Violet.

The last time they had seen each other, they were two years old. They were practically babies.

But now they were in kindergarten.

Mabel hoped that the two five-year-olds would get along. Mya liked gymnastics; Violet liked magic. . . .

Right there was a big problem.

Would Violet keep her magic secret from Mya? Mabel hoped that she had warned her about it strongly enough during "the Talk."

Mabel hoped their cousins weren't nosy, like her friend Simone.

If Violet did let a little magic slip out, she

hoped they wouldn't stare and point. Or tell their parents.

Or even worse — *hers*.

Still, there was one lucky thing: Mya and Zoe were her father's relatives. No magic on *that* side of the family!

Mabel would only have to worry about *one* person's magic on this trip. And that was quite enough.

"We're here!" her father announced, turning down a tree-lined road.

"Hooray!" Violet yelled. She threw a bunch of candy wrappers into the air. They fluttered down on the seat and floor.

"Violet," Mabel said. "I bet Mya doesn't throw candy wrappers all over the backseat."

Her little sister stuck out her tongue. "You don't know that!"

Ahead of them was a big yellow house. Mabel's stomach began to churn nervously.

"I can't *wait* to get out of this car," their mother said.

"Me, neither," their father said. He turned into the driveway.

"Where's Mya?" Violet asked eagerly. "I want to go swimming with her."

"Tomorrow," their mother promised as the car came to a halt.

As Mabel fumbled with her seat belt, Violet shot out of the car.

The front door opened and two girls rushed from the house to meet them.

The older girl, Zoe, was wearing cutoff jeans and a T-shirt. A baseball cap perched on her head. Her hair was cut short, almost like a boy's.

The younger one was dressed in pink shorts and a frilly top. She was cute and tiny, like a dancer.

She pranced down the driveway and came to a halt in front of Violet. The two five-year-olds stared at each other.

Mya grinned. There was a big gap in the middle of her mouth. "I just lost a tooth," she said to Violet. "Wanna see it?"

She and Violet grasped hands and ran into the house together.

Oh dear, Mabel thought. They hadn't been here for more than a few moments, and already she had broken her vow to keep her eye on Violet.

But Mabel couldn't watch Violet every single second. Could she?

She got out of the car. She and Zoe looked at each other shyly.

Their parents were greeting one another.

"Jerrold!" Mabel's father exclaimed. "Susanna!"

"It's been way too long," Mabel's mother said.

Zoe began to toss a baseball into the air and catch it.

Mabel felt awkward. Should she join in? Or not?

"Are you hungry?" Susanna asked. She put an arm around Mabel's mother's shoulder.

"We had dinner on the road," she replied. "But I'd love a cup of tea."

"Mabel?" Susanna said. "Do you want something to eat or drink?"

Mabel shook her head.

"Zoe, show Mabel to her room."

"*My* room?" Mabel repeated. She felt a sudden panic. Had they given her a room without Violet?

Zoe threw down the baseball. "Come on," she said. She led Mabel into the house.

"This is *my* room," she said proudly, opening a door.

Her room had posters of baseball players and koala bears. There were clothes on the floor and books on the bed.

It's a mess, Mabel thought. But she tried to be polite.

"Nice posters," she said. She was glad she didn't have to sleep there.

"Thanks," Zoe said. She led Mabel into the hall again.

"And here's Mya's room." Zoe flung open the door to an even messier room, decorated in pink and white and lavender.

"And here's where you and Violet are going to sleep," she said.

"Me and Violet?" Mabel let out a sigh of relief.

She glanced at the two single beds made up with plaid blankets. A small shelf held paperback books.

It was clean and neat. And Mabel had her own bed.

"It looks very nice," she said to Zoe.

Zoe sat down on one of the beds. "Are you a good swimmer? Can you swim in deep water?"

"Sure," Mabel said. "I love to swim. We have a pool in our backyard."

That was because of Violet's magic, of course.

Zoe looked pleased.

"We're going to the beach tomorrow,"

she said. "You and I can swim out to the dock together. There's a diving board and everything."

"What about Violet and Mya?"

"Our little sisters will have to stay in the shallow end."

Mabel couldn't help feeling anxious. "But who will watch them?"

"Our parents, of course," Zoe said.

Mabel frowned. She wasn't sure she wanted her parents to watch Violet. But luckily, her mother still didn't have a clue. Neither did her father.

Her parents had no idea what Violet had done on the road.

That was because Mabel had been there. She had explained and covered up.

They were still the same happy family they had always been.

And Mabel wanted to keep it that way.

Violet's magic hadn't changed anything important in their family — except that Mabel worried all the time.

Weren't *adults* supposed to be the ones who worried?

Mabel sighed. She wanted nothing more than to get away from her little sister for a few hours.

But she just couldn't do it.

Chapter Six

"I can swim," Mya announced. She flopped on her back and splashed wildly. Then she scrambled to her feet.

"Can *you* do that?" she dared Violet.

Violet ducked underwater and came up spluttering. "See? I can do *that*," she announced.

"Look at this!" Mya said. She stood on one leg in the water. Then she struck a ballet pose.

In answer, Violet grabbed Mya around the waist. She lifted her up. "I'm very strong!" she bragged.

Zoe nudged Mabel. "Aren't they adorable?" she said.

"Sure," Mabel agreed.

Violet hadn't done magic all morning. Last night, before they went to sleep, Mabel had given her another Talk.

So far, it seemed to be working.

"Do you want to race to the dock?" Zoe asked.

She was wearing a sleek racer-back bathing suit with cool turquoise goggles. Her short hair was damp and stuck up in spikes on her head.

She looked trim and athletic and cute.

Mabel was glad she had a new navy polka-dot bathing suit. She felt cute, too — though not as athletic as Zoe.

"Shouldn't we keep an eye on the girls?" Mabel didn't want to get too far from Violet.

"That's what parents are for." Zoe pointed to their mothers, who were sitting together on a blanket on the sand.

"They might want to play games with us."

"So?" Zoe said. "I don't want to hang around with little kids all day."

Was it safe? Mabel wondered. Could she leave Violet?

But her sister was on her best behavior. Maybe it wouldn't hurt to go off with Zoe for a while.

Zoe dove into the water and headed toward the dock.

After a moment, Mabel followed her.

Mabel hauled herself out of the water and shook herself off like a seal.

"Now let's race to that buoy," Zoe said, pointing.

Mabel hesitated. It was the sixth time they had raced. Zoe had won every contest.

"Come on. It'll be fun," Zoe urged.

Mabel adjusted a strap on her new bathing suit. She had to admit that even though Zoe was a better swimmer, she was having fun.

A *lot* of fun.

Her cousin didn't boast or brag. She kept encouraging Mabel.

She encouraged her now. "You're a really good swimmer," she said. "If you lived here, you could join the swim team."

"I'm not very fast," Mabel said.

"But you're strong," Zoe insisted. "You'd be a great distance swimmer."

"Really?" Mabel had never thought of herself that way.

She liked the thought.

Usually she just splashed around in the pool. From now on, she was going to do laps, strong and steady.

"Let's go," Zoe said. She stood at the edge of the dock, ready to dive in the deep water.

The two girls dove in.

The wind was high and the waves were choppy. Water kept crashing into Mabel's face. But she swam as steadily as she could.

Ahead of her, Zoe moved like a dolphin through the water.

She was ahead, like she always was.

"I'm a distance swimmer," Mabel repeated to herself. She reached the buoy just a few minutes after Zoe did.

They turned around and swam back to the dock.

"Let's do it again," Zoe said as they climbed onto the dock.

Mabel tried to catch her breath. She had pushed herself to keep up with Zoe.

She pulled off her goggles. "In a minute," she said.

The two girls sat down on the dock, dangling their feet in the water.

"That was really great," Zoe said.

"Yeah," Mabel agreed.

"I wish you lived near us," Zoe said. "You could join the swim team and meet all my friends."

Mabel smiled.

"We'd have sleepovers all the time," Zoe continued. "We're cousins, so our parents wouldn't say no."

"And I'd teach you to bead."

"Cool!" Zoe said. "We'd make friendship bracelets."

"I wish I had brought my beads," Mabel said. "I left them at home."

"Next year," Zoe said.

Mabel wrote a silent memo to herself. *Remember to bring beads on next visit to cousins'.*

She hoped it would be soon. Very soon.

Mabel closed her eyes and let out a long breath. She couldn't remember when she had last felt so relaxed.

Zoe began to list all the things they would do together if Mabel lived nearby.

"We'd visit the fair in September; we'd sled and ice-skate in the winter; we'd sing in the school chorus together. . . ."

"You've got everything planned," Mabel said approvingly.

She loved plans. She loved schedules. She loved organized activities.

Zoe smiled. "I wish it would all come true."

Mabel shielded her eyes from the sun and peered at the shore. "What do you think Violet and Mya are doing?"

She hated to bring up the subject, but she had to ask.

"They're over there in the shallow end," Zoe said. "Tossing the orange ball. Aren't they sweet together?"

"Yeah," Mabel agreed.

The ball flew higher and higher. "I wonder if they're daring each other again," Mabel said.

Zoe suddenly sat up straighter.

"What is it?" Mabel asked in alarm.

Then she saw it. A heavy orange-tinted cloud was rolling in over the lake. Flashing colored lights streaked around it.

There were rumblings of thunder that sounded almost like laughter.

Mabel's heart began to pound.

The cloud was almost the same color as the ball that Mya and Violet batted back and forth.

Had Violet forgotten everything Mabel had told her? Was she showing off her magic to Mya?

The lifeguard blew her whistle. "EVERYONE OUT OF THE WATER," she shouted through a bullhorn.

"CLEAR THE SWIMMING AREA IMMEDIATELY."

Mabel jumped to her feet.

She didn't say a word. She didn't wait for Zoe. She dove into the water and headed straight for shore.

Mabel needed to get to Violet before she did any more damage.

Chapter Seven

On the beach, Violet sat huddled under a beach towel with Mya. The two girls were shivering with cold.

Their hair hung in long wet curls. Their fingertips were blue. They had just gotten out of the water.

Colored lightning flashed in the sky above them.

As Mabel hurried toward the girls, she saw Violet lift her arm.

"Watch this," Violet said to Mya.

She pointed one blue, wrinkled finger at the lake. Balls of blue, orange, and rose light began to glide over the water.

Mya giggled. "More," she said.

Violet made the lights bounce on the waves. Then she stood up.

"BECAUSE OF DANGEROUS WEATHER CONDITIONS," the lifeguard announced, "THE SWIMMING AREA IS CLOSED FOR THE DAY."

Mabel didn't know what Violet was going to do next. But she knew she had to stop her.

She planted herself in front of her sister. "Cut it out!" she hissed.

Violet's eyes seemed glazed. They focused on a faraway point. Her breathing had quickened.

"Do you hear me?" Mabel said loudly. She stamped her foot. "Enough!"

Violet blinked. She shook her head. Then she glanced apologetically at Mya. She snapped her fingers.

Instantly the storm clouds lifted. The lightning slowly faded. The colored lights twinkled and disappeared.

"Violet," Mabel began in a serious voice.

She drew in a long breath. She had a lot to say.

And she couldn't wait to say it.

But Violet didn't stick around to hear the lecture. She grabbed Mya's hand and ran away laughing.

Mabel bit her lip. It was probably all her fault, anyway.

For a short time, she had relaxed. She had forgotten her little sister. She hadn't bothered to watch out for her magic.

And look what had happened! Violet had practically shut down a state park.

She had ruined the afternoon for a *lot* of people. Including Mabel.

"Hey," Zoe suddenly said from right behind her.

A towel was slung around her shoulders. Her hair was dripping and her feet were wet.

How long had she been there?

"You are *fast*!" Zoe cried.

"What?" Mabel said. Was she talking about Violet? Mabel hadn't been fast enough.

"I can't believe the way you dove off that dock. You were practically flying," Zoe continued. "If our swim coach saw you, she'd sign you up today." Zoe looked curiously at Mabel. "Why were you in such a hurry?"

"I wanted to get back to Violet," Mabel said, "to, um, make sure she was, um, okay...."

Zoe moved closer. "I saw," she whispered.

Mabel tried to keep herself calm. "Saw what?"

"You know."

"Um, no," Mabel said. Her heart thudded inside her chest. "I don't."

Zoe's face flushed. She glanced down at her feet. "I'm sorry," she said.

"For what?" Mabel was starting to feel sick inside.

"I overheard you and Violet late last night," Zoe said. "And I heard you talking . . . about Violet's magic, I mean."

For a moment, Mabel thought she was going to faint.

No one had ever come close to knowing about Violet and her magic. No one had ever guessed. Not even her nosy friend, Simone.

Mabel could barely look at her cousin. "Were you spying on us?"

"Of course not!" Zoe cried. "It was a total accident. I was just passing your room. . . ."

She must have overheard Mabel giving Violet the Talk again.

A lot of good *that* had done, Mabel thought.

"You shouldn't have listened," she said to her cousin.

"I couldn't help it," Zoe apologized. "And anyway, I didn't think it was real until I saw the orange fog."

She looked at Mabel. "Is it true? Does Violet really have magic?"

Mabel tried to control the fear and panic sweeping through her.

She didn't know what to do now that the secret was out. It was funny; she hadn't planned for it at all.

At least Zoe was a member of the family. Did that make a difference? Mabel hoped so. She liked Zoe and she wanted to trust her.

"Yes," she admitted. "It's true."

"I've never known anyone with magic before." Zoe's eyes sparkled. "And you're my cousins!"

"It's Violet who has it, not me," Mabel said. She took a deep breath. "Have you told anyone?"

"Not a soul."

"Good," Mabel said. "Can you keep it a secret?"

"Of course!" Zoe cried.

Mabel leaned closer. "My mother

can't find out," she said. "It would kill her."

"You can count on me," Zoe said.

The two girls shook hands.

"What about Mya?" Mabel asked in a sudden panic. "Will she tell?"

Mya and Violet had joined their parents at a picnic table on the other side of the beach.

"She won't say anything. If she does, everyone will think she's making it up,"

Zoe said. "She's always saying crazy things."

"Violet, too," Mabel said. "Only her crazy things come true."

"Tell me more about her magic!" Zoe begged.

"She enchants carrots, um, flies around her bedroom, and makes animal noises come out of the piano," Mabel said. "It's been one disaster after another."

Although that wasn't completely true. Her sister's magic had helped a lot during their aunt's wedding.

And thanks to Violet, they now had an Olympic-size swimming pool in their backyard.

It was *mostly* one disaster after another.

"And you don't have *any* powers?" Zoe said again. "That can't be right."

"It's true," Mabel said. "Violet got them all. I didn't get anything."

Chapter Eight

"What a shame that bad weather blew in," Susanna said. "The day started out so well!"

"The cloud had a strange orange tint," Mabel's mother said. "Do you think it was pollution?"

Mabel and Zoe exchanged glances.

"Good thing our sisters are in the other car," Mabel whispered.

After the beach had closed for the afternoon, the two families decided to drive into the city.

"You'll like the botanical gardens," Susanna said to Mabel's mother as they turned off the highway. "It's one of the main attractions here."

Zoe rolled her eyes. "Bo-ring!"

"You and Mya can show your cousins the giant insects," her mother said.

"That'll take ten minutes," Zoe grumbled. "There's nothing else to do except look at flowers."

"You can take them to see the cactuses," Susanna suggested. "Or the greenhouse. Or the Japanese gardens."

Zoe and Mabel both groaned.

"Those things are for grown-ups," Zoe complained. "Not for us."

"But grown-ups deserve to have fun on vacation, too," Mabel's mother said. "Don't you agree, Susanna?"

"That's right. You kids can entertain yourselves for an hour," Susanna said. "Mabel and Zoe, stay with Violet and Mya. We'll keep our eyes on you."

"Oh, great," Mabel muttered under her breath.

Boredom plus Violet. *That* was a recipe for disaster if she ever heard one.

Mabel drew in a long breath. She hoped that her sister was done with magic for today.

"There are too many flowers here!" Violet complained as the four cousins wandered through the gardens.

"But they're so pretty!" Mabel said. "And they smell so good!"

The gardens were better than she expected.

There were masses of brilliantly colored flowers. There were wooden bridges over small streams. There were shady, tree-lined paths.

Violet wasn't having any of it. She stuck out her lower lip. Her curly hair fell over her face.

"I hate it," she said.

"Me, too," Mya said.

"I'd rather be playing baseball," Zoe agreed.

"Can we visit the bugs?" Mabel interrupted. "It's not every day that we get to see supersize insects."

It would make a great essay subject for school, Mabel thought. She'd try to memorize a few facts. Her teacher would be so impressed!

She began to walk down the path. "Come on," she called. "It'll be more fun than complaining. I *promise!*"

To her relief, Zoe followed her. And then the two little girls did, too.

The four cousins walked over a bridge. They passed a bed of purple flowers and came to a stop in front of a small pond.

In the middle of the pond was a dragonfly.

It was about ten feet tall. It was shiny and polished, with huge dark transparent wings.

"Wow," Mabel breathed. She had never seen anything like it.

Violet started jumping up and down. "I want to climb on it. I want to ride that flying dragon."

"It's a dragonfly," Mabel corrected. "And you can look, but you can't touch."

"But I want to!" Violet said, as if that changed anything.

"Sorry," Mabel said. She stared at the dragonfly. It was like something out of a science fiction movie.

It looked like a dinosaur, only not as scary.

Mabel tried to imagine giant dragonflies moving slowly through the botanical gardens, or maybe flying over the water like small planes.

It would be a great start for her essay. . . .

Half an hour later, they had seen all the bugs.

They had seen the cactuses and the greenhouse and the tropical plants.

They had checked in with their parents a bunch of times.

They had wandered around the botanical gardens and watched Mya and Violet turn cartwheels on the lawn.

Mya still looked perfectly clean, but Violet had grass stains on her knees and hands.

How did she manage it? Mabel wondered. Her little sister could get dirty in a bathtub.

She made Violet wash off her hands. Then they sat on a bench to wait for their parents.

"I liked the ant best," Mabel said to the other girls. "Which was your favorite bug?"

"Ladybug." Mya leaned against her big sister. For the first time that day, she looked tired. "I want to go home now."

"Soon," Zoe said to Mya.

"My favorite bug was the grasshopper," she added.

"I liked the flying dragon," Violet announced.

"Dragonfly," Mabel corrected again.

"Whatever." Violet jumped up. "Can I run to those trees?"

"Stay where I can see you," Mabel warned.

Before she could say another word, Violet raced down the path.

"I want an ice-cream sandwich," Mya said.

Zoe searched in her pockets. "No money," she said. "Wait until Mom and Dad get here."

"But I want one!" Mya said. She kicked her legs.

"I have money," Mabel offered. She took out her change purse and began to count out quarters and dimes. "Here. Get whatever you want," she told Mya.

Mya skipped to the ice-cream wagon.

"Thanks . . ." Zoe began to say.

"Look!" she said urgently. She pointed to the sky.

Mabel lifted her eyes.

A small craft was flying over the botanical gardens.

It wasn't a bird and it wasn't a plane. . . .

It was a dragonfly.

And Violet was seated on its back.

Chapter Nine

I should have known that this would happen. That was the first thought that flashed across Mabel's mind.

Mabel's fingertips and toes tingled as she stared at her sister high above the treetops.

She didn't want to think about what would happen if Violet fell. Hopefully her magic powers would save her.

After all, Violet had flown before, at least in her bedroom. It wasn't quite the same, though.

Mabel had another fear, too: What if an adult saw Violet? What if it was one of her parents? Or a policeman?

Violet was probably breaking dozens of laws.

She might even get arrested for stealing the dragonfly.

That wasn't important, though. Violet's safety was.

We can't startle Violet, Mabel thought. *We have to get her down! Now!*

And no one must see her.

Zoe stared openmouthed at the sky. "I can't believe this!" she whispered. "It's totally awesome. I hope Mya gets back in time to see."

Mya was still at the ice-cream stand. Mabel hoped she would stay there.

"It's not awesome!" Mabel cried. "It's scary! What if it was your little sister up there?"

Zoe's smile faded. "I'm sorry," she said.

"What am I going to do?" Mabel cried.

It was all so crazy.

How could Violet, who was afraid of the

dark, get on the back of a statue and fly a hundred feet in the air?

How could Mabel, so far away, get Violet to land safely?

"Can you talk her down?" Zoe said.

"She's up too high up to hear me."

"Try, anyway," Zoe said. "It might work."

The dragonfly begin to rise higher in the air. In a minute, her little sister might disappear altogether.

"Come on," Zoe said. "You can do it."

Mabel drew in a deep breath. She squared her shoulders.

It was worth a try.

It might be her only hope.

"Come down, Violet," she whispered.

High above her in the sky, Violet was laughing wildly. Her feet were bare. Her hair was blowing around in the wind.

"Down!" Mabel commanded. "Come down."

Was it her imagination or did the dragonfly start to move downward?

"Keep on going," Zoe said.

Mabel concentrated. She closed her eyes and pictured the dragonfly heading toward the pond.

She said the word *down* three times.

She imagined the dragonfly landing gently.

She pictured Violet safely on solid ground again.

"It's working!" Zoe cried. "You did it!"

Mabel opened her eyes.

She hadn't really done anything — Violet was too far away to hear her.

She had gotten very, very lucky.

Maybe, through a miracle, she had managed to reach her little sister — or maybe Violet had just decided to come down.

She looked at Zoe. She looked at Mya, who had just returned with an ice-cream cone.

"I saw Violet in the sky," Mya announced.

"Shush!" Mabel said. She looked to see if other people had heard or noticed. But there was no one else around.

"Come on!" Zoe said.

The three cousins began to run toward the dragonfly pond.

They found Violet on the lawn. She was gazing at the dragonfly.

Maybe she couldn't believe she had just flown it.

Or maybe she was thinking about flying it again.

It was back in the pond. No one could tell that it had recently been airborne.

There was no trace of the recent flight.

Unless you counted Violet's very windblown hair, her slightly wet clothing, and her bare feet.

"Violet!" Mabel gasped.

She rushed over to hug her little sister.

Zoe and Mya were close behind her.

"Don't do that again!" Mabel cried. "We were so scared! And where are your sandals?"

"They fell off somewhere," Violet said with a shrug.

Her eyes sparkled. "I saw the tops of trees! I was next to the clouds! You looked like ants!"

Mabel put her hands over her face. She was starting to feel dizzy again.

"You flew! You flew!" Mya cheered Violet.

Mabel put her fingers to her lips. "Hush," she said. She wished that Mya would be quiet about it.

She wished that she wasn't so excited about Violet's flight.

But Mya was only five years old. She couldn't help it.

"This is a secret," Zoe said.

"Yes," Mabel agreed. "That goes for both of you. You can't tell any—"

Violet pulled away from her and rushed across the lawn. "Mommy!" she cried.

Their parents had arrived.

Chapter Ten

"Guess what we found," Jerrold said as they made their way to the parking lot.

"Ice cream?" Mya said.

"Man-eating flowers?" Zoe said.

"Flying dragons?" Violet asked.

Mabel didn't say anything. She couldn't stop thinking about Violet in the air.

What if she had fallen?

What if she had flown away?

What if she had refused to come down?

It was so lucky that everything had worked out.

"Mabel?" Jerrold interrupted her thoughts. "Do you want to guess what we found?"

"Um, a cactus?" Mabel said.

"You're all wrong," he said cheerfully. He glanced at Violet's bare feet. "Missing something, partner?"

He dangled a pair of lemon-yellow sandals in the air. Then he tossed them to Violet.

"We found one on the east and the other on the west side of the garden," he said.

"You girls got around," Susanna commented.

"Um, yes," Mabel said. She glanced at Zoe.

"We covered a lot of ground," Zoe said.

And a lot of sky, Mabel silently added.

"Mabel and Zoe, you did a good job looking after your sisters," Mabel's mother said. "I knew that we could count on you."

Mabel usually loved to hear compliments like this. But today it just didn't feel right.

She should have stopped Violet from flying. She shouldn't have let her get off the ground.

Flying the dragonfly was the most dangerous thing her little sister had ever done. Mabel hadn't watched her closely enough, and she'd almost landed in real trouble.

Later that evening, when their sisters were in bed, Mabel and Zoe went into Zoe's room.

They made themselves comfortable on pillows. Zoe brought out a bag of potato chips.

"I've been thinking," Zoe said, taking a handful of chips. "About Violet and her magic."

"What?" Mabel leaned forward eagerly. "I need all the help I can get."

"What if you have powers, too?" Zoe said.

"I wish," said Mabel.

"No, really," Zoe insisted. "You can stop Violet's magic cold."

"Very funny!" Mabel said.

"You stopped her twice today," Zoe said. "Once at the beach and once at the gardens."

Mabel shook her head. "That was luck or coincidence or a miracle or aliens. It had nothing to do with me."

"I don't agree," Zoe said.

"You've got it all wrong." Mabel glanced at her cousin. "I don't mean to hurt your feelings," she added quickly.

Zoe didn't look hurt. She ran her fingers through her short hair. Then she smiled.

"I'll give you ten dollars if you don't have powers," she said.

"Do you enjoy losing?" Mabel asked.

"Do you enjoy winning?" Zoe retorted. "You win, either way. If you don't have my allowance, you'll have magic."

Mabel groaned. *"I don't have magic,"* she said. "Why won't you believe me?"

"Oh, admit it already," Zoe said.

"There's nothing to admit," Mabel said. "And, frankly, having magic isn't all that great. It causes trouble, makes messes, and gets people very upset."

Zoe didn't answer. She jumped up and began to clean off the bed.

"What are you doing?" Mabel asked a little nervously.

"Clearing a space on the bed," Zoe said. "So you can fly off it."

As Mabel stared at her, Zoe said, "It's only a foot or two to the floor! You won't get hurt!"

"You're out of your mind," Mabel said. She picked up the bag of chips. "Here. Eat some more chips."

Zoe pushed them away. "No, thanks." Then she went over to the door and locked it.

"This is going to be a scientific experiment," she said. "No one will know about it except us."

"No," Mabel said.

"Yes," Zoe said. She slipped off her sandals and climbed on the bed.

After a moment, Mabel followed her.

"How will I know if I'm flying or falling?" Mabel asked.

"By whether you feel heavy or light," Zoe said.

"Really?" Mabel wasn't so sure if she'd notice the difference.

And she felt silly, standing on the edge of the bed with her arms spread out and her feet bare.

She closed her eyes.

"Your body is becoming weightless," Zoe murmured. "You are light as a feather. You are floating into the air. . . ."

THUMP! Mabel tumbled off the bed and fell heavily onto the floor.

"Ouch," she said.

"I think you're getting the hang of it," Zoe said.

"I'm *not*," Mabel said, rubbing a sore spot on her leg.

"Try again," Zoe said.

This time, Mabel kept her eyes half open. She imagined herself soaring through the room. She jumped. . . .

And she jumped. . . .

And . . .

"Okay, forget about flying," Zoe said as Mabel picked herself up for the sixth or seventh time. "We still have lots of magic powers left."

Mabel rolled her eyes. "I tried one power," she said. "And all I have to show for it are bruises and bumps."

"Why don't you try turning yourself into a mouse?" Zoe suggested.

"No way!" Mabel said. She picked up her sandals. "I'm going to bed now."

Zoe blocked her path to the door. "Just one more experiment, Mabel," she begged. *"Please!"*

"Oh, all right," Mabel said.

Zoe pointed to her baseball cap on the desk. "Make it move!" she said.

"What's the point?" Mabel said.

"Come on, you have to believe!" Zoe said.

"Why me?" Mabel groaned. But she shut her eyes and held her palm over the baseball cap.

"Anything happening?" she asked after a minute or two.

"Not yet," Zoe said.

Mabel circled her hand over the cap. "Does this help?"

"Not really," Zoe said.

She opened her eyes. *"I don't have magic,"* Mabel said. "Do you believe me now?"

There was a loud knock on the door.

Mabel and Zoe looked at each other.

"Mabel?" Violet said. She rattled the handle. "Unlock the door. I want to come in."

"Zoe and I are busy now," Mabel said. "Go back to bed."

"Open the door!" Violet said.

"Not now," Zoe said. "Didn't you hear Mabel?"

The handle began to move. The lock clicked open. Violet was using magic to enter the room.

Mabel's eyes flashed. "No, Violet!" She held up her hand. *"Stop!"*

The door hinges creaked. The door seemed to sigh. Then the lock clicked back in place.

From the other side of the door, Zoe and Mabel heard Violet's footsteps running down the hallway.

The door of the guest room slammed.

The two cousins exchanged a long look.

Zoe smiled triumphantly. "Do you believe me now?" she said.

Chapter Eleven

Mabel sat on her bed in the dark.

Across from her, Violet was sound asleep. The covers were thrown over her face. She was snoring quietly.

Mabel aimed a flashlight at a notepad on her lap. She was doing something she loved to do, especially when she was confused, upset, and alone.

She was writing a list.

MABEL'S MAGIC — A REPORT CARD

1. Flying: F
2. Shape-shifting: F

3. Spell-casting: F
4. Vanishing into thin air: F
5. Mind reading: F
6. Stopping Violet's magic: A

Mabel put down her pen and sighed. If she *did* have magic powers, they were definitely linked to Violet's.

Just her luck. Why couldn't she have her own, separate magic?

"Whatever," she muttered.

Mabel thought back. There were many, many times when she had tried to stop Violet's magic.

Once her sister had made piles of sweaters rise up and dance in her father's store.

Had Mabel stopped her then?

Maybe.

Once Violet had made moving pictures appear on the wall of Mabel's third grade classroom.

Had Mabel stopped her?

Probably.

And once Violet made baby carrots turn colors and fly around the kitchen.

Had Mabel put a stop to it?

Almost certainly.

If she thought about it, Mabel had probably stopped Violet's magic dozens of times.

How had she missed seeing it?

And why hadn't Uncle Vartan said anything?

Did he just like to keep her guessing? Or did he want her to figure it out by herself?

"You'd think he'd have tipped me off," Mabel muttered under her breath. "It would have been nice."

Mabel felt a rush of gratitude toward Zoe. She had discovered her magic only because of her cousin.

She'd "lost" the bet. But when she got home, she would buy the most beautiful beads she could find and make a friendship bracelet and matching necklace for her.

If Mabel really had magic, that is . . .

She still wasn't one hundred percent convinced that she did.

There was only one way to be sure.

She had to ask Uncle Vartan.

He was the one person who would know.

But how could she reach him?

In the past, she had slipped letters

to him inside the pages of a magical fairy-tale book.

But the fairy-tale book was hundreds of miles away.

Mabel didn't want to wait until they returned home. She wanted Uncle Vartan's answer *now*.

She flicked off the flashlight and sat in the dark, thinking.

A few minutes later, she stood up and tiptoed to her suitcase. She opened it up and shined a light inside.

Mabel pulled out a plastic bag. Inside were the postcards she had brought with her.

She selected one with a picture of a fat pink rabbit on the front.

Dear Uncle Vartan,
Please answer these questions:
1. Do I have magic?
2. Is it true that I can stop Violet's magic?

3. *Do I have any other powers?*
4. *What are they?*

P.S. Violet flew on a dragonfly. It was dangerous.

There was no more room on the postcard. Mabel squished her signature in the corner.

Then she breathed a sigh of relief.

She felt better now that she had written to Uncle Vartan.

But she still didn't know how to get the message to him.

She couldn't give the postcard to her parents.

The fairy-tale book was far away.

And she didn't have Uncle V's telephone number. It probably changed all the time, anyway.

Mabel glanced at her little sister. Violet was still sleeping soundly.

She quietly slipped the postcard under Violet's pillow.

Maybe she would find an answer in the morning.

Mabel climbed under the covers of her bed. As she closed her eyes, she thought she saw a silvery light fill the room.

Then she fell into a deep, dreamless sleep.

Chapter Twelve

Yes.

It was one, single, glittery, shimmery, silver word.

The word was written on a postcard.

It lay on the floor between Mabel's bed and Violet's.

As Mabel leaned over to pick it up, she wondered how it got there.

Had Uncle Vartan snapped his fingers to send it?

Had he asked a bird to carry it across the country?

Or had he simply made it appear?

Mabel grasped the edges of the card.

As soon as she touched it, it began to dissolve.

The word Yes glimmered for a moment, then disappeared.

Mabel was left holding nothing.

There was a bit of silver dust on her fingertips. She blew it off.

"Typical Uncle Vartan!" Mabel muttered.

He had given her an answer. That was something.

He hadn't said "No," or "Forget about it," or "You must be kidding."

But Mabel was still confused.

To which question had he answered "Yes"?

Did she have powers? Could she stop Violet? Did she have other magic powers, too?

Mabel glanced at her little sister.

Violet was still asleep. She looked so sweet and innocent.

It was hard to believe that yesterday she

had flown above the treetops, with her feet bare and her hair wild.

What mischief was she going to do today?

But I can stop her, Mabel reminded herself. *I think I can. At least, it's likely that I can.*

Or maybe Uncle Vartan's "Yes" meant that she should just keep on trying?

Somehow, Mabel felt more confident. She felt peaceful. She felt strong.

As the day wore on, she felt better and better.

Was that magic? Or was it just the magic of believing in herself?

That day, Violet didn't do any magical mischief.

They swam at a neighbor's pool, and Violet didn't enchant the flippers or the air mattresses or the water toys.

She didn't make the water pink or polka-dotted or bright green.

She didn't turn anyone's swimming goggles into snorkels.

Was it because Mabel had discovered her own powers?

Or was Violet saving up her magic until later?

The best part of the day was yet to come.

Tonight, the cousins were going to camp out in Zoe and Mya's yard.

They were going to sleep in a tent. They had sleeping bags, camping mattresses, and flashlights.

No one would tell them when to go to sleep. They could stay up all night if they wanted.

They could eat candy and play cards until three in the morning.

They could go outside and dance around the yard in their pajamas.

Maybe they'd even see the sunrise.

Mabel couldn't wait.

*   *   *

"If you need us, we're right here," Mabel's father reminded them for the sixth or seventh time.

"We *know*, Dad," Mabel said.

She glanced at the sky. It was a perfect night for a campout. There was a full moon and no clouds. Leaves rustled in the warm breeze.

The girls had put on their pajamas. They had brushed their teeth and washed up.

Mabel had a lantern in her hand. Zoe was carrying a cell phone and a flashlight. Violet had a bag of books and games, and Mya was holding several stuffed animals.

"We're ready," Zoe announced.

"Will there be bears?" Violet asked a little nervously.

"No bears," Zoe reassured her.

"Foxes?" Violet said. "Wolves? Tigers?"

"None," Zoe said.

"The mosquitos are what you have to watch out for," Jerrold said. "Get into the tent and zip it up tight."

"Okay," Violet said in a small voice.

"Don't worry, Violet, Zoe and I will protect you," Mabel said. "We'll make sure that you're safe."

"That's right," Mabel's mother said.

"Listen to your big sisters," both sets of parents told the little girls.

"Be good to your little sisters," they told the older girls.

"And don't make yourself sick on candy," they added.

"Try to get some sleep," Susanna said.

"Have a good time," Mabel's father said as the girls walked down the porch stairs and began to cross the yard.

Mabel held the lantern up for her sister and cousins. Then she crawled into the tent and zipped it shut.

The girls looked at one another.

They were on their own.

Chapter Thirteen

Mya knew exactly what *she* wanted to do. "Fly, Violet!" she said, clapping her hands. "Fly!"

Violet looked around the inside of the tent.

"Oh, no you don't," Mabel said quickly. She wasn't going to let her sister do that again.

Especially not at night, when Violet could disappear out the tent door and into the darkness.

"That's right," Zoe backed her up. "Don't even think about it."

"Okeydokey." Violet snapped her fingers.

Suddenly the tent was filled with tiny, darting lights. There were fireflies everywhere.

Mabel brushed them away. At least they were harmless. "Violet," she sighed. "Get rid of them."

"Keep them," Mya said.

"I will," Violet said. "So there."

Mabel glanced at Zoe. The fireflies clustered at the top of the tent. They weren't bothering anyone.

It wasn't worth picking a fight over them.

"Never mind," Mabel said. "Let's all get along and have a good time."

"Let's tell ghost stories," Zoe said. She made herself comfortable on her sleeping bag and took out some candy.

Mya moved closer to her big sister. "Tell us the one about the ghosts and haunted house," she said.

Violet scowled. "I don't like ghost stories," she said.

"Sit next to me," Mabel offered, patting her sleeping bag. "I'll protect you."

"No," Violet said, sulking. "I want to eat candy."

Zoe tossed her a chocolate bar.

As it flew through the air, it grew bigger and bigger.

Mya screamed with delight.

An enormous chocolate bar landed on Violet's lap. It burst through its silver wrapping paper and broke into dozens of pieces.

"Want some?" Violet offered.

Mya grabbed a handful.

"You'll make yourselves sick," Mabel warned as the two little girls stuffed magical chocolate into their mouths.

"We won't," Violet said, opening her mouth wide to show off her chocolate tongue.

Fireflies swooped down and landed in her mouth. They melted along with the chocolate.

"Do it again!" Mya cried.

It's going to be a long night, Mabel thought.

But, so far, the magic wasn't hurting anyone. Mabel wasn't going to stop a little harmless fun. As long as they kept it to themselves.

"We have to keep all the magic secret," she told them. "Do you understand, Mya?"

Mya nodded.

"Ready for a ghost story?" Zoe asked.

"No!" Violet said.

Mya leaned over to whisper in Violet's ear. Violet nodded. The two five-year-olds exchanged secret smiles.

What now? Mabel thought.

"We're ready," Mya announced.

Zoe cleared her throat. "There was once a haunted house," she began. "It was filled with cobwebs and bats and spiders. . . ."

Violet sneezed.

"Cover your mouth," Mabel said.

When Mya started giggling, Mabel looked up. There were cobwebs hanging from every corner of the tent.

But, luckily, no spiders or bats.

Zoe went on with the story. "Late one night, someone started banging on the door," she said.

She rapped three times.

"Who's there?" Mya said.

"Meeeeee . . ." Zoe said in a spooky voice. "Let meeeeee in."

Violet sneezed again.

The zipper on the front flap of the tent slowly began to unzip itself.

A gust of cold wind blew into the tent.

"Oooh," Mya squealed in delight.

"I'm coming in," Zoe said.

The tent flap opened. And then it closed.

"I don't want to hear any more ghost stories!" Violet burst out.

"Cover your ears," Mabel said. "The rest of us want to hear it to the end."

"And then, you'll never guess what happened next. . . ." Zoe said.

"No!" Violet cried. She snapped her fingers twice.

A clearing appeared in the tent. Logs were arranged neatly in the center.

Right before the girls' eyes, they burst into flame.

"Cool!" Violet breathed, delighted by her own magic. "Awesome!"

"Where are the marshmallows?" Mya cried. "Let's make s'mores!"

Zoe held her hands over the fire. "Hey, this thing is real," she said, looking a bit alarmed.

"What have you done now, Violet?" Mabel cried. "You can't play with fire! Get rid of it!"

"But I like it," Violet said. She picked up a stick and speared a marshmallow.

"She's right, Violet," Zoe said. "Put the fire out. It's dangerous."

Violet gave the marshmallow to Mya. Then she speared another one for herself. "No," she said.

Zoe picked up a bottle of water and poured it over the fire. But the flames didn't go out.

"It's magical," Zoe said. "Do something, Mabel!"

Violet snickered as Mabel snapped her fingers.

The campfire flickered and then it burned more brightly than ever.

"Violet, this is not funny," Mabel said. "The tent might burn down. Someone could get hurt."

"It won't," Violet said, "and you can't make me."

"Actually, I can."

Violet shook her head.

Mabel pointed at her sister. *"Stop it. Now."*

The fire whooshed up.

Mabel clapped her hands.

The flames swooped down. Then they slowly shrank. With an angry hiss, they disappeared into the earth.

Only a charred spot remained in the middle of the tent.

Zoe threw her arms around Mabel. "You did it!" she cheered. "Your magic worked! Hooray!"

"But my s'more . . ." Mya cried, staring at her marshmallow. "It's not done yet."

Violet was pale. "You didn't do that," she said to Mabel.

"I did," Mabel said. She smiled. "Are you going to be more careful now?"

"You don't have magic," Violet retorted. "Only I do."

"Do you want to try me?" Mabel challenged.

For once, Violet was silent.

Mabel blew a bit of ash from her fingers. "Maybe we should skip the ghost story," she said to Zoe. "What about a nice game of cards for everyone?"

About the Author

Anne Mazer grew up in a family of writers in upstate New York and remembers waking up every morning to the sounds of two noisy electric typewriters. She loved books so much that she would sometimes read up to ten books in a single day! She is the author of forty books for young readers, including The Amazing Days of Abby Hayes series and the award-winning picture book *The Salamander Room*. To learn more about Anne, visit her at www.AmazingMazer.com.

Meet eight-year old,
one-of-a-kind, ultra-fabulous
Ruby Booker!

She sings like nobody's
business, has a pet iguana,
and dreams of being a
famous animal doctor!

If you enjoy the sneak peek of the first book, be sure
to check out all the books in the series!

Here is a sneak peek at
Ruby and the Booker Boys #1:
Brand-new School, Brave New Ruby

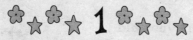

1
Rise, Shimmy, and Shine

I woke up at 7:15 in the morning.

The first day of school was *really* real when my clock radio went off at 7:30. Ma had fixed it the night before to play my favorite song, "Cotton Candy Clouds," a let's-get-going-and-have-a-good-first-day-of-school song.

The coolest group in the world, the Crazy Cutie Crew, sings that song. They only have three members. But I like to pretend I'm the fourth.

As soon as the first note hit my ears, I stood up on my bed like it was a stage (even though Ma doesn't like me to). I sang every single word, really loud, as if the Crazy Cutie Crew wrote the song for me:

"When the sun hits the clouds
And rainbows kiss the sky,
A sweet wind blows,
And then I know
That today is mine, all mine."

This is pretty much how I begin each morning. I sing so loud, the rest of my family uses *me* as an alarm clock.

I leaped onto the floor and hit a perfect landing on my super-soft rug. It looks

like big piano keys. But instead of the keys being boring black and white, they are purple and orange.

"Cotton Candy Clouds" was bouncing off every wall in my room when I slid over to my window. I pulled back my curtains and got the biggest hug from the sun. Those morning rays covered my face with a color that's hard to find in a crayon box. If happy was a color I guess that's what I would call it.

Before I knew it I heard someone coming down the hall outside my bedroom door.

It was Ma and my three big brothers, Ro, Ty, and Marcellus. When they got to my room, they were all rubbing their eyes and yawning. From the smell of sausages and eggs floating into my room, I could tell that Daddy was downstairs making breakfast.

"We hear you, Ruby. Loud and clear, baby. Loud and clear," Ma said with her big, pretty smile. She picked me up and squeezed me real warm and tight, just like she does every morning.

"Girl, do you know how early it is? Are you part girl, part rooster?" Ro asked angrily. "You sure do crow loudly."

"Yeah, ladybug," my biggest brother, Marcellus, added. He calls me ladybug. I like it. That name fits me, because I'm cute and I like to think that I bring good luck wherever I go. "We all love your singing, Ruby, and we're used to it, but this is extra, extra early."

"What else do you all expect? That's Rube. It's what she does," my third brother, Ty, said with a grin. He took his glasses out of the pocket of his pajama top, popped them on his button nose, and then said, "Good morning, Rube. Sounds like you're ready for school." He always says nice things to me. I love me some Ty.

"Okay, boys, leave your sister alone. Let's get ready and head downstairs for breakfast," Ma said, pointing down the hallway toward the boys' rooms. "And you, Miss Superstar Third-grader, you said you wanted to pick out your own outfit this morning. So get to it, sister!" Ma poked my belly. She loves tickling me.

As far as my clothes go, orange and

purple rule. Before I went to bed, I hung my first-day-of-school outfit over the chair at my desk. It was a brand-new orange-and-purple shirt, a brand-new jean jumper, long orange-and-purple-striped socks, and to top things off, my favorite shoe combination. One orange sneaker and one purple. I couldn't wait to put everything on to show Ma.

After washing up, brushing my teeth, and putting on my purple-and-orange perfection, I grabbed two bracelets. Purple and orange, of course. And I put on my favorite pretend pearl earrings. Then I pressed repeat on my radio alarm clock and sang "Cotton Candy Clouds" even louder. I heard Ro screaming from down the hallway, "GIVE US A BREAK, RUBY!"

I love to get on his nerves.

As I looked in the mirror for the last time, I whispered to myself, "Ruby Marigold Booker, you sure are fabulous!" And that's the truth.

There's Magic in Every Book!

The Rainbow Fairies
Books #1-7

The Weather Fairies
Books #1-7

The Jewel Fairies
Books #1-7

The Pet Fairies
Books #1-7

The Fun Day Fairies
Books #1-7

Come flutter by Butterfly Meadow!

#1: Dazzle's First Day

#2: Twinkle Dives In

#3: Three Cheers for Mallow!

#4: Skipper to the Rescue

#5: Dazzle's New Friend

#6: Twinkle and the Busy Bee

WHERE EVERY PUPPY FINDS A HOME!

THE **PUPPY PLACE**
Where every puppy finds a home

GOLDIE

THE **PUPPY PLACE**
Where every puppy finds a home

SNOWBALL

ELLEN MILES

THE **PUPPY PLACE**
Where every puppy finds a home

SHADOW

ELLEN MILES

SCHOLASTIC

READ THEM ALL!

SCHOLASTIC
www.scholastic.com
SCHOLASTIC and associated logos are trademarks and/or registered trademarks of Scholastic Inc. **PUPBL**